THIS BOOK BELONGS TO:

Hopkins

For Dave
~A.H.B.

For Jamie and Joseph
~G.W.

ISBN0-439-23713-0

12 11 10 9 8                                                    3 4 5 6/0

Printed in the U.S.A.                    08

First Scholastic printing, September 2001

# Little Mouse and the Big Red Apple

### A.H. Benjamin and Gwyneth Williamson

SCHOLASTIC INC.

New York  Toronto  London  Auckland  Sydney
Mexico City  New Delhi  Hong Kong  Buenos Aires

Mouse was feeling hungry one day when all of a sudden he came across a big red juicy apple.

"Just what I want!" he cried. "I'll take
it home with me and have a feast!"

Mouse set off towards his little house,
rolling the apple over and over.

He couldn't wait to get his teeth into
the big red juicy apple. "Yum, yum,"
he thought, when all of a sudden . . .

SPLASH!

the apple rolled into a pond.
"Oh no!" wailed Mouse. "What am
I going to do now?"
"Not to worry," said Frog, popping
his head out of the water. "I'll help
you."

Frog kicked the apple hard with his strong back legs. It flew out of the water, and . . .

# BUMP!

landed on the ground.
"There you are," said Frog.
He licked his lips and stared
at the apple.

"Er, thanks," said Mouse, as he began to roll it along the path. He did not want to share his apple with Frog. Mouse went on his way, thinking of the lovely apple dinner he would have later. His mouth was already watering when . . .

CRASH!

the big red juicy apple
fell into a thorn bush.

"Silly me!" muttered Mouse,
as he tried to rescue his dinner.
"Ouch, that hurt!" he cried.
"Those prickles are nasty!"

"I see you have a problem," said Tortoise,
moving next to Mouse. "Leave it to me."
Tortoise didn't have to worry about
the sharp prickles. He had his shell to
protect him.

Without any trouble
at all, Tortoise crept under
the thorn bush and brought
out the big red juicy apple.
"Problem solved!" he said, stroking
the apple longingly.
"I'm ever so grateful," said Mouse in
a hurried voice, and he was off again.
He did not want to share his apple
with Tortoise.
"I'll soon be home and biting
into that big red juicy apple,"
thought Mouse,
when . . .

the apple rolled into a log.
"That's all I need!" sighed Mouse when
he saw that the log blocked his path.
"How do I get round that?"

"Easy!" said Mole, popping out of a nearby hole. "I'll dig you a tunnel."

And she did. She dug a tunnel that went right under the log.

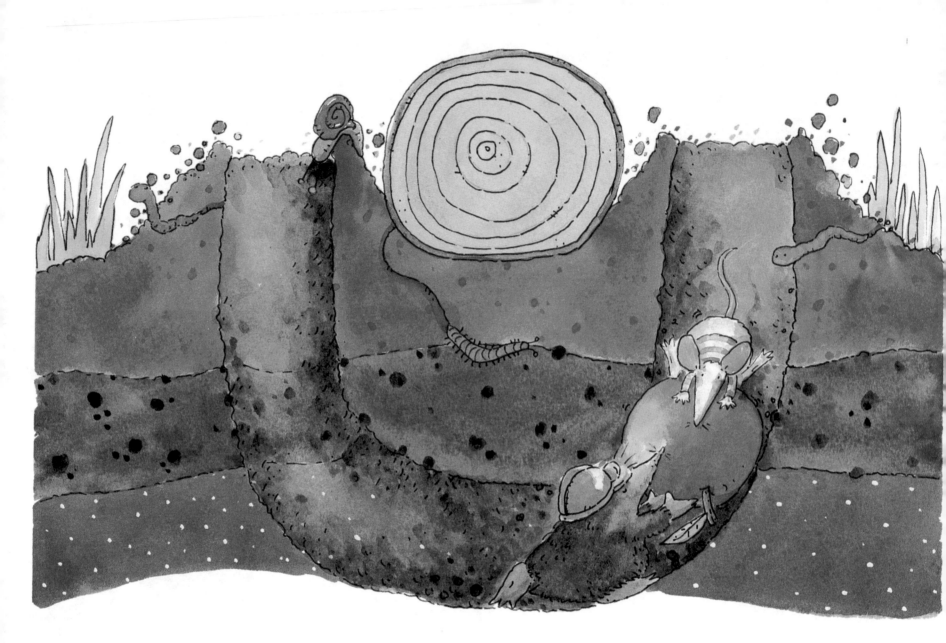

It was just wide enough for Mouse
and the apple to go through it.

"Always glad to help!" said Mole, sniffing at
the big red juicy apple with her little nose.
"It's very kind of you," said Mouse, and he
went on his way as fast as he could. He did
not want to share the apple with Mole.
He rolled the apple over and over until . . .

he came
to a steep hill.
His house was at
the very top.

PUSH

Push, push,
heave, heave,
went Mouse,
grunting and
groaning.

PUSH

HEAVE

HEAVE

Up, up, up
he went,
until he reached
the very top.

"At last!" sighed
Mouse happily.
"Oh for that lovely
apple meal!" But, as
Mouse let go . . .

the apple wobbled,
and then it started
to roll . . .

down the
other side
of the hill!

It rolled
faster and
faster...

further
and further,
until...

it came to a stop at the bottom
of the hill. Mouse could see
it lying there, like a big
red jewel.
"Oh no," he cried,
"I'll have to start
all over again!"

Mouse scrabbled down the hill on his little
tired feet. Faster and faster he ran . . .

but when he reached the bottom
he found Frog, Mole and Tortoise
had got there first!
"How kind of you to send that
apple all the way back to us,"
called out Mole, chomping
away on a piece of it.
Mouse gave a big, big sigh.
"Don't mention it," he said.
"Isn't that what friends are for?"